KT-460-844

TEAM
HERO

Cardiff Libraries
www.cardiff.gov.uk/libraries

Llyfrgelloedd Caerdydd
www.caerdydd.gov.uk/llyfrgelloedd

CARDIFF
CAERDYDD

ACC. No: 07033704

Special thanks to Michael Ford

ORCHARD BOOKS

First published in Great Britain in 2018 by The Watts Publishing Group

1 3 5 7 9 10 8 6 4 2

Text © 2018 Beast Quest Limited
Cover and inside illustrations by Dynamo
© Beast Quest Limited 2018

Team Hero is a registered trademark in the European Union
Series created by Beast Quest Limited, London

The moral rights of the author and illustrator have been asserted.
All characters and events in this publication, other than those clearly in the public domain,
are fictitious and any resemblance to real persons, living or dead, is purely coincidental.

All rights reserved.
No part of this publication may be reproduced, stored in a retrieval system, or transmitted, in any form
or by any means, without the prior permission in writing of the publisher, nor be otherwise circulated in
any form of binding or cover other than that in which it is published and without a similar condition
including this condition being imposed on the subsequent purchaser.

A CIP catalogue record for this book is available from the British Library.

ISBN 978 1 40835 206 9

Printed and bound by CPI Group (UK) Ltd, Croydon, CR0 4YY

The paper and board used in this book are made from wood from responsible sources.

Orchard Books
An imprint of Hachette Children's Group
Part of The Watts Publishing Group Limited
Carmelite House, 50 Victoria Embankment, London EC4Y 0DZ

An Hachette UK Company
www.hachette.co.uk
www.hachettechildrens.co.uk

TEAM HERO

ANDROID ATTACK

ADAM BLADE

ORCHARD

SPECIAL BUMPER BOOK

MEET TEAM HERO ...

JACK

POWER: Super-strength
LIKES: Ventura City FC
DISLIKES: Bullies

RUBY

POWER: Fire vision
LIKES: Comic books
DISLIKES: Small spaces

DANNY

POWER: Super-hearing, able to generate sonic blasts
LIKES: Pizza
DISLIKES: Thunder

CONTENTS

STORY 1

THE MAN'S face was invisible under the helmet as he worked with a welding torch. Orange sparks arced through the air and scattered across the floor of the laboratory.

He turned off the jet of flame and stopped for a moment, lifting the visor and staring up at the array of monitors on the wall above him. Each screen showed a surveillance feed from the different Team Hero outposts around the world. He chuckled to himself. *They don't even know they're being watched! They don't know what's coming ...*

The man took a step back to admire

his creation — a robotic arm the size of a tree trunk, clad with a metal alloy that could withstand a blast from any weapon known to man.

"Just one more piece," he said. "Soon, you will rise!"

And when my work is complete, the world will be ours ...

CHAPTER 1

CYCLOPS SECURITY

JACK'S GRIP was sweaty on the hilt of his sunsteel sword, Blaze. He peered around the corner of a wall, trying to spot his enemy in the gloom of the warehouse. They'd been locked in combat for almost half an hour already.

Where are you?

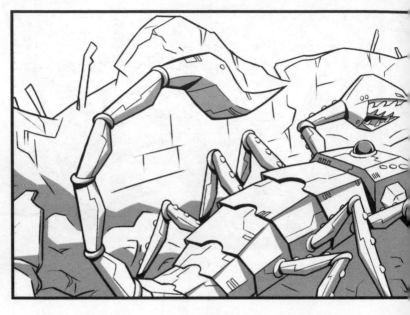

The wall above his head exploded
as a giant pincer smashed through.
Jack rolled out under the falling
debris, then stood to face the attack.
The giant robotic scorpion, two
metres long and scurrying on six legs,
came after him, its bulbous stinger

glowing an angry red. Its metal shell
was scarred with dents and scratches
where Jack's blade had found its target,
but it didn't seem to be slowing down.
Whenever Jack thought he might be
getting the better of it, it came back
with a surprising new attack.

Out in the open, he had nowhere to run as the stinger powered up. He waited until the last possible moment before diving aside. The laser beam sliced through the air and scarred a path across the concrete floor.

"You missed again!" Jack shouted, charging in and slicing at the robot's legs, where its hydraulics were exposed. But this time, the leg retracted completely inside the main shell, and so Jack missed, stumbling past his enemy just as the scorpion ducked its head and rammed him, sending him skidding across the floor. He tried to stand, but his enemy placed a sharp foot on his chest and pressed him to the ground. Another pincer grabbed his wrist and tried to twist the sword out of Jack's grip. He fought back, focusing on the power in his scaled hands, watching them glow a golden colour, but the scorpion's stinger shot down and stopped a fraction from his forehead.

"Do you submit?" said an electronic voice.

Jack thought about punching the contraption in the head.

"I calculate a laser beam at this range would fry your brain," said his Oracle, Hawk, through the earpiece Jack

wore. *"I would admit defeat if I were you."*

Jack sighed and let Blaze drop to the ground.

"You win," he muttered moodily.

"Deactivate!" Jack heard a human voice call out.

The robotic scorpion stepped off him and backed away, its red eyes fading to black as it powered down. Lights flickered on across the Hero Academy training warehouse, revealing an upper gallery filled with students and teachers. With all his focus on the fight, Jack had managed to forget that all of Team Hero had been watching the battle.

Great — everyone just watched me get humiliated!

He picked up Blaze and sheathed it.

A young man wearing jeans, a black hoodie and spectacles descended a set of stairs from the gallery to Jack's level. His name was Areevo Vaste, and he was the owner of Cyclops Security,

the world's most advanced robotics company. He was here to show off some of their latest technology. Jack's friend Danny said Areevo had become a billionaire by the time he was twenty-one. Jack didn't know if that was true, but Areevo was often featured on the covers of science magazines, and had had dinner with the President on more than one occasion. He was one of the most recognised faces on the planet.

Areevo also happened to be a graduate of Hero Academy, a school for gifted individuals dedicated to fighting evil around the world.

"Thank you for the demonstration, Jack," he said warmly.

"You mean thanks for losing to your robot," Jack replied.

Areevo laughed. "I'm afraid that was always going to be the conclusion of the exercise."

Jack clenched his fists in frustration. He didn't like Areevo's tone. "Let me have another try," he said.

The Cyclops boss patted the giant metal arachnid. "It wouldn't end any better for you," he said.

From the gallery, Ruby called down. "Well, how about me?"

"I'll take it on!" added Danny.

One by one, the other students raised their hands, all wanting a turn.

Areevo called for quiet. "I think you've misunderstood," he said. "I have the greatest respect for all of your abilities, but this scorpbot isn't just a mindless attack droid. It has my new Scorp-X AI chip implanted."

"AI as in artificial intelligence?" asked Professor Rufus. The squat, red-haired tech teacher looked like he was trying to contain his excitement at seeing Areevo's creation in action.

"That's right, Professor," said Areevo. "It learns, storing every action taken against it, and cross-referencing with every other attack it has seen, and every attack others in its nest have seen. As you fight, it adapts to your behaviour and responds accordingly. You're not just fighting a brainless droid, but a hive-mind supercomputer. After just a few minutes, it knows what you're going to do almost before you do!"

Jack thought about how the scorpbot had improved as the fight went on, and how the leg had retracted to protect itself. *So that's what was going on ...*

On the gallery, Chancellor Rex, headmaster of Hero Academy, began to clap. "Well, I'm impressed, Areevo," he said, beaming with pride. Areevo had been his student at the Academy only a few years before. "This sort of technology could give Team Hero the edge in our fight against evil."

Jack looked at the looming scorpbot beside him. For some reason, the thought of fighting alongside robots made him feel a little uneasy.

"Now, I have a few more things to show you that we've been working on," said Areevo. "Why don't you all come down and see?"

The students began to file from the gallery. Danny and Ruby walked over to Jack's side.

"Never mind, man," said Danny. "It's just a robot. Take out the batteries and it's as useless as an old tin can."

"Thanks," said Jack. His pride was still bruised, but thanks to Danny, it hurt a bit less.

Areevo resumed his demonstration. He opened a cupboard and took out an electric guitar. Then he strummed a note. Jack heard a buzzing in the air, and a cloud of black drones dropped from the ceiling above. They stopped in mid-air, hovering in a spherical swarm about three metres across. Areevo plucked another string

and the ball began to make its way towards the group of students. Jack made out that the individual drones were bat-shaped.

As the note rose in pitch, the swarm sped up, faster and faster. Jack felt a prickle of panic — he and his fellow students were right in its path. One or two of his schoolmates began to take a step back.

As the swarm reached them, Areevo played a sharp power chord and the sphere of drones exploded into a looser formation. Jack watched the drones zip past at a remarkable speed, almost brushing his face. The crowd gasped aloud, some covering their heads in fear. At a low twang from Areevo's guitar, the swarm came together again on the other side, this time in the shape of a single unblinking eye — the Cyclops Security logo. He then played another chord and the batbots ascended back to the ceiling.

"That's amazing!" said Ruby. "You controlled them with music."

"It's just one method," said Areevo, putting the guitar down. "At Cyclops, we get all our inspiration from nature. The drones exist as individuals and as part of a collective network. They work together and learn together using the same Scorp-X technology as the attack bot Jack faced." He turned to Rufus. "I think I've shown off enough of my toys for today. Perhaps I could have a word outside, Professor? We could chat about Team Hero's requirements."

As they left the warehouse through a side door, Danny picked up the electric guitar, shouldering the strap. "I've always wanted to be in a band," he said.

"Er ... Danny, perhaps now isn't the—" Jack began.

Danny strummed a discordant

note, and the batbots dropped and swarmed over Chancellor Rex. He flailed his arms wildly, trying to shaking them off.

"Oh no!" said Danny. He tried another string, and this time the bats seemed to latch on to the Chancellor's clothing, lifting him into the air.

"Danny! Get them off me!" he roared.

"I don't know how!" said Danny.

Jack grabbed the guitar from his friend, and tried to remember the chord Areevo had played. He'd had a few lessons, back home in Ventura City, before he came to Hero Academy. *If I get this wrong, who knows what they'll do?*

He placed his finger on a fret and played the chord. The batbots dropped Chancellor Rex in a heap and shot back to their resting places above.

Phew!

The headmaster got to his feet, his face as grey as his hair, and glowered at Danny. "I'm going to get some air. Please, Daniel, do not fiddle with anything else."

As soon as the Chancellor had gone, everyone burst out laughing.

"For someone with super ears, you're terrible at music," said Ruby.

"Do you think I'll get detention?" asked Danny. "Surely Chancellor Rex will see the funny side!"

As he spoke the words, their headmaster appeared at the door. His face was anything but amused.

"All faculty members outside at once," he said. "Come quickly!"

Jack and the others followed as the Chancellor led a band of teachers to an alleyway running behind the warehouse.

There was no sign of Professor Rufus or Areevo Vaste.

But Chancellor Rex pointed at something on the ground. Stepping nearer, Jack saw it was a shattered Oracle device. All of the pupils and staff from Hero Academy wore them — the Oracles could access information instantly, and also give those wearing them a variety of enhanced sight filters like infrared and X-ray vision. And one of the first things they were taught was not to take them off. The Oracles also emitted signals allowing them to be traced.

"Is it Professor Rufus's?" asked Danny.

"I'm not sure," said the Chancellor, looking grave, "but it seems likely."

"And look at this!" said Ruby, bending down to pick up a pair of bent spectacles.

Those are Areevo's!

Jack, Ruby, and Danny exchanged shocked glances.

What happened to them?

CHAPTER 2

SABOTAGE

BACK IN the Hero Academy Command
Centre, faculty members and officers
manned their workstations, searching
for the missing men. Several hours
had passed since Professor Rufus and
Areevo Vaste vanished. Jack and his
friends stood with Chancellor Rex as
the security feeds from the time of the

disappearances were routed to the main monitor. The screen was blank.

"It's the same with all the cameras," said Danny. "Something blocked the signal for the crucial time period."

Jack was feeling helpless. It was as if Rufus and Areevo had simply vanished from existence. None of the guards had seen anything amiss. None of the fences had been breached. There was no path of evidence to follow. *We're completely in the dark.*

"Areevo's special power is channelling electricity," Rex said. "If they were attacked, he might have defended himself with a pulse that shorted out the feeds."

"Or someone switched them off," said Ruby. "This was a well-planned operation by someone who must have had some insider knowledge."

Jack agreed with his friend.

How else could someone infiltrate Hero Academy itself?

Suddenly, warning lights flashed across the Command Centre, and the air filled with the wail of a siren. A monitor exploded with a shower of sparks, and an officer jumped back, crying out as his control panel crackled with electricity.

On another screen Jack saw reams

of code flashing.

"We're being hacked!" said the technician. He began to type frantically. "It's not a program I'm familiar with."

"Can you fight it?" asked Chancellor Rex.

Other officers jumped on to machines, working quickly to battle the software attack.

In Jack's ear, Hawk began to sing, *"Humpty Dumpty sat on a wall. Humpty Dumpty had a great—"*

"What are you talking about?" Jack asked.

Hawk switched to a language that

sounded like Japanese.

Ruby took Kestrel, her Oracle, out of her ear. "It's some sort of virus," she said. "It's affecting all our systems."

Jack muted Hawk, just as he was sharing a recipe for Duck à l'Orange.

One by one, the computer screens across the room went blank.

"Everything's compromised!" shouted an officer. "Whoever's doing this has complete control of our systems."

"How can we stop them?" asked Danny.

"Get to the main servers in the basement," said Rex. "There's a manual shutdown function."

Jack and his friends sprinted towards the doors of the Command Centre, just as red lights flashed all around. An automated voice calmly intoned, "Initiating security overrides. Blast door containment."

A huge reinforced steel door began to descend in front of them. "Quickly!" shouted Jack, pumping his legs harder. He flung himself through with Ruby at his side, but Danny tripped and sprawled underneath the massive, heavy door.

"Help!" he cried.

Jack reached for him. With one

hand, he used his super-strength to
slow the door. And with the other
hand, he grabbed Danny's wrist,

pulling his friend through just before his body was crushed. With a *clang*, the blast door slammed down.

"Thanks!" said Danny.

Jack surveyed the huge door. "We're on our own now," he muttered.

Though much of the Academy was filled with high-tech apparatus, the fortress's original buildings dated back almost a thousand years, so they had to take a narrow stone staircase down to the cellars, rather than the main lifts. They were all breathing heavily when they arrived at the arched door to their destination.

The servers were huge wardrobe-sized blocks of plugs and wiring. The main lighting was down, but the servers twinkled with red and white lights, illuminating switches and cables. The air was cool. At first, nothing looked amiss, but Danny paused at the door, ears twitching. "I hear something ..."

Jack unmuted his Oracle. "Hawk, switch to infrared vision."

"The weather in Acapulco is a balmy twenty-eight degrees," was the only reply.

"Great," muttered Jack, before telling the others. "Still scrambled."

The three friends pressed further

into the room. Now Jack could hear something too, over the air-conditioning — an odd chittering and tapping sound. It seemed to be getting closer. He drew Blaze from the scabbard. Danny unshouldered his energy bow. Between them, Ruby's eyes glowed deep red, armed with fire-beams.

Jack sensed movement to his left and jerked his head to see. A shadow scurried between the servers and disappeared out of sight again.

"Hello?" said Jack. "Is someone down here?"

"Jack, look!" whispered Ruby. She was pointing upwards, to the top of one of the servers, where something with beady orange eyes perched. As it arched its bulbous tail, Jack realised it was a scorpbot. It wasn't nearly as large as the one he'd done battle with in the training ground though. This one was no bigger than a household dog.

"It looks sort of cute," muttered Danny.

The scorpbot spread its front pincers and its stinger began to whirr — it was armed with some sort of electric drill bit.

"Cute?" said Ruby. "If you say so. Why don't you try stroking—"

The droid leapt through the air, straight at Danny's face. He squealed and lifted his arms, but Ruby's fire-beam met the creature a moment before it hit. It landed on the ground, still burning, legs squirming until it lay still.

"Yeah, really cute," said Ruby.

"Maybe there was only one," said Jack.

"Like we've ever been that lucky," said Danny.

Five more scorpbots emerged among the server blocks.

He just had time to wonder what they were doing down there when two more bots launched themselves towards him. He sliced the first in two in an explosion of sparks, and smashed the second aside with the flat of his blade. Danny pinned one to the wall with an energy arrow and it fizzled out of life. Jack turned and saw Ruby frying one with her eyes, then pinning another with the edge of her shield. A third was poised to attack her, but Jack pounced and stabbed it through its metal shell. He felt the air above him stir, and saw a bot dropping for his head. With no time to swing his sword, he dropped into a crouch, but the scorpbot never landed on him. He heard Danny's booming sonic cry and the scorpbot shot through the air and thudded into one of the servers.

"Thanks, man," Jack said.

The room was still, and filled with smoke from the wrecked bots. But chittering sounds still came from the electronics around them.

"There are more," he said, leading the way onward. "Keep your eyes peeled."

Peering around one of the servers, he saw what had to be the mainframe — a towering console with several screens. Three scorpbots crawled over it. One had a pincer inserted into a socket, and the others were tearing out wiring from inside.

Jack signalled to the others with his

fingers. *Take one each.*

They both looked at him open-mouthed, frozen in horror.

What's the matter with them? It's only three little robots.

Then he realised.

"There's one right behind me, isn't there?"

They both nodded, and Ruby lifted her shield. In its mirrored surface, Jack saw a scorpbot clinging to the server block at his side, its stinger poised a few centimetres from his ear. As the drill bit began to whirr, he punched the scorpbot with his golden hand, shattering it into pieces.

The bots clustered around the
mainframe shot towards them. Ruby
sprayed an arc of fire across two,
and Danny impaled the last with an
energy arrow. For a moment, everyone
was breathing heavily as they waited

for the next attack.

"I think that's all of them," said Ruby.

They turned their attention towards the mainframe. It didn't look good at all. All the lights were off, and frayed wiring spilled from the inside.

"They destroyed it completely," said Danny, inspecting the damage closely. "Where did they come from?"

Jack crouched to examine the remains of one of the bots. Behind its head parts, it bore a logo in the shape of a red eye.

"Cyclops Security," said Ruby, echoing Jack's thoughts.

"That makes no sense," said Danny. "Cyclops is on our side."

"Maybe not," said Jack. "Think about it. Who had the ability to disrupt all the security feeds, to hack our systems?"

"You're not saying—?" Danny began.

"Areevo Vaste," said Ruby grimly. "He's a genius who would know Hero Academy systems inside and out."

Jack nodded. "Don't you think it's weird, the Professor and Areevo vanishing like that? We didn't hear a fight, or even any sound. What if it was planned from the start?"

"If you're right, then how can we

find the Professor?" asked Ruby.

Jack looked at the smoking carcass of a scorpbot, and it gave him an idea. "Areevo said all the bots are connected. If we can isolate their command signal, we could follow it back to its source. Find out where Areevo is hiding."

Ruby gestured at the destruction around them. "Good luck finding a computer that works around here."

"What about *Arrow II*'s systems?" Danny suggested. "It's not connected to the mainframe."

Arrow II was the name of the Academy's fighter plane. The original had been destroyed but there was an updated version in the hangar. It had never been flown.

"Good thinking," said Jack. He shared a worried glance with his friends. With the blast doors down, everyone else was trapped in the Command Centre.

It's up to us.

CHAPTER 3

ARROW II

THEY KEPT their weapons out and ready as they made their way through the deserted corridors of the Academy, just in case their enemy sent any more scorpbots. They reached the hangar, where the sleek form of *Arrow II* sat on the launchpad. Rumour had it that the new and improved craft could break the sound barrier. On board, they went through the hold area and into the cockpit, where they located the communications array. Ruby found a cable to link up the dead scorpbot's CPU. They scanned through the menus to find the command signal history, and it gave them a set of co-ordinates locating the last signal received. It was hundreds of miles away from Ventura City, deep within a region of desolate rocky canyons.

"That's where the Cyclops HQ is," said Ruby.

Jack nodded. "It's our best bet. And it makes sense that Areevo would

take the professor to his home turf."
He looked at the control panel. "How
many flying lessons have you had?"

Ruby grimaced. "Two."

"Two's better than none," said Jack.

"Both in a simulator," added Ruby.

"Does that mean you can fly this
thing?" asked Danny.

Ruby strapped herself into the
pilot's seat. "It means I can try."

Jack and Danny took the two
co-pilots' chairs. Ruby's fingers
danced over the switches, bringing
Arrow II online. The craft vibrated as
the engines roared into life.

"We have a problem," said Danny,

nodding through the windshield. "With the mainframe down, there's no way to open the hangar doors."

"I've got it," said Ruby, pulling up a joystick. She pushed the button on the top and a missile streaked from under the nose of *Arrow II*. It exploded into the hangar doors, and as the smoke cleared, Jack saw open sky beyond.

"Rex is going to put us in detension until we're forty," said Danny.

Ruby flicked several more switches on the dashboard and the ship's engines rose in pitch.

"Ready for lift-off?" she said.

Jack nodded nervously. Danny's fingers gripped the armrests of his chair.

Ruby pulled the lever sharply and *Arrow II* shot out of the hangar so fast Jack was pressed back into his seat.

He felt like his whole skeleton was being crushed. The nose of the aircraft rose and they climbed towards the sky above, before levelling off at twelve thousand metres.

"That was fun," croaked Danny. "And terrifying at the same time."

"Plotting a course for Cyclops HQ," said Ruby, using a touch-activated map-screen. *Arrow II* banked and pushed through the clouds.

They crossed miles of open ocean before reaching the forests of the mainland. Gradually, these gave way to barren hills of bare rock. The famously secretive Areevo Vaste had built his base miles from anywhere. *Miles from help too*, thought Jack.

They'd been travelling at nine hundred knots for several minutes, when Danny pointed to several dots on the radar screen — something was in the airspace dead ahead.

"Should we be worried?" he asked.

"Probably," said Ruby. "They're twenty kilometres out and closing at our altitude."

"Nineteen kilometres," Jack corrected her. "Eighteen. Seventeen ... looks like they're on an intercept course."

"Taking manual evasive manoeuvres, twenty degrees to starboard," said

Ruby. Hands on the steering column, she steered right. On the radar, the dots adjusted too.

"Fourteen kilometres," said Jack. "Looks like they're only small objects. Bird-size."

Ruby tried to change course again, but with the same result.

"Ten kilometres," said Jack. "They're moving faster than us, so we can't outrun them. I say we go straight through them."

"Agreed. Holding course for intercept," said Ruby. "Seven kilometres, six, five, four, three, two, visual ..."

Jack saw them through the windshield — they did indeed look like a small flock of black birds. And at the last moment they broke apart. *Arrow II* nosed through the open space they left. The dots on the radar vanished.

"Where'd they go?" asked Danny.

Sudden bangs and creaks sounded from across the plane, and on the control panel a diagram of the craft started flashing in multiple locations. "We've got hull breaches!" said Ruby.

A spinning black buzz-saw broke through above their heads, casting sparks across the dashboard.

"Drones!" cried Jack. The flying droid dropped into the cockpit, and righted itself. It looked like a black seagull, but its wings were serrated metal and it had a single red eye. As soon as it saw Jack, the eye glowed brighter. Jack jumped aside, drawing

Blaze as a laser bolt tore past and
fizzled into the side of the cockpit.
He drove the sunsteel point through
the drone's chest and it spasmed
and collapsed. More crashing sounds
came from the back of the plane.
Jack opened the door back into the

hold area to see more drones cutting through the fuselage. He closed it again.

"How's it look?" asked Danny.

"Not good," said Jack. "How far are we from the Cyclops campus?"

"Thirty kilometres out," said Ruby.

The aircraft lurched to port, and Ruby fought with the steering column. On the diagnostic display, one wing was illuminated orange. "Engine one's down," Ruby said. "The drones are sabotaging the ship."

"We need to destroy them," said Jack. "All hands on deck. Let the autopilot take over for now."

Ruby set the controls and stood up, eyes already glowing with readiness for the fight.

Jack stood by the door. "On three. One, two, three!"

He flung open the door on to a scene of smoke and carnage. The drones were causing chaos, with crisscrossing laser beams sizzling over the cargo deck. They'd already sawed huge holes in the fuselage, and the space howled with air from outside. Jack stepped in, slicing and cutting at anything that moved. Ruby's fire-beams lit up a drone in mid-air, and Danny shot arrow after arrow, crisping the flying bots on contact.

Ruby spun around, a drone clamped to her shield's surface. She ran hard into the fuselage, crushing the bot between the shield and the wall. It fell off, shaking its head dizzily, then Jack chopped it clean in half. There were no more that he could see.

"I think we got them all," he said, breathing hard.

With a judder, the sounds of the plane suddenly went quiet.

"That's engine two gone," said Ruby. "The autopilot will try to glide us in, but I'd suggest you both buckle up — we're in for a bumpy landing."

There were safety harnesses lining the laser-scarred walls of the hold, and they quickly fastened themselves in. A low-tone alarm was sounding, counting down the altitude. Though the gaping holes in the fuselage, Jack saw red rocks flashing past, covered in scrubland. *We're going too fast! We're going to—*

He didn't even hear the crash before everything went black.

CHAPTER 4

RESCUE ABORTED

"ARE YOU OK?"

The voice sounded distant, like it was coming from underwater. Jack tried to speak, but all that came out of his mouth was a groan.

"You've had a knock on the head," the voice added. "Don't try to move."

Jack felt something cold and

soothing against his temple. Light filtered through his eyelids and he opened them to see two kind faces looking down. A man and a woman, about the same age as his parents. They smiled warmly.

"What happened?" asked Jack.

"You were in a crash," said the man. "We heard it from our ranch."

Suddenly it all came rushing back. *Arrow II*. The drone attack. The engine failure ...

Danny ... Ruby ...

Jack sat up sharply, and it brought a wave of sickening dizziness.

"Hey, stay put!" urged the woman.

But Jack was panicking. All around him, pieces of smoky wreckage lay strewn across the rocky ground. Above them on either side rose a steep red canyon. He couldn't see Danny or Ruby anywhere.

"Your friends are fine," said the man. "Maxi's looking after them."

"Who's Maxi?" asked Jack.

Right then he saw Danny and Ruby walking over with a small girl of about eight. Ruby's tunic was torn at the shoulder and Danny's hair looked like he'd put on his gel in a hurricane, but they were otherwise unhurt.

"Are you OK?" asked Ruby.

Danny reached to help Jack up.

"I think so," said Jack as he found his balance. He felt pretty good considering he'd just been in a plane crash. "Where are we, Hawk?"

His Oracle replied with a series of

bird sounds, before Jack remembered the mainframe had been scrambled. He put his Oracle on mute again.

"Not sure who Hawk is," said the man, pulling a map from his pocket. "But we're right here." He pointed to a spot in the middle of nowhere, among mountains and desert. There was a red dashed line encircling an area of several acres.

"What's that?" asked Danny.

"All that land is owned by Cyclops Security," said the man.

"Perfect!" said Jack, climbing to his feet. "That's where we were headed."

"You sure?" asked the woman

doubtfully. "We could take you to the nearest town. It's only an hour away."

Jack glanced at his friends. The drone attack could only mean one thing. *Areevo knows we're coming.*

"We're sure," he said.

The family's All-Terrain Vehicle was parked up nearby and they squeezed in alongside Maxi. She was looking at Danny with a frown.

"What's with your ears, anyway?" she said, as they set off and bumped over the landscape.

"Maxi!" said her dad. "Don't be rude."

"It's all right," said Danny. "I was born this way," he told the girl.

Jack tried to hide his scaled hands, but she'd already seen them. "Your eyes are funny too," said the girl, pointing at Ruby. "Kind of orange."

Ruby grinned. "You've never seen anyone with orange eyes before?"

"Sorry about Maxi," said her father. "She's just young."

They continued for another ten minutes, before the mother spoke.

"That plane looked pretty high-tech. Who did it belong to?"

"My parents," said Jack quickly. "They work at Cyclops." He looked out of the window, but everything around them looked the same. *Cyclops HQ*

looked close on the map.

"Are we nearly there?

He caught the father's eyes in the mirror. They too were slightly strange — grey, but almost silver. "We have to take the long way round to avoid the creeks," he said. "We'll be there soon.

So, your parents let you fly a plane on your own?"

Jack wasn't surprised at the question. Who wouldn't be curious about three kids crash-landing in the desert?

But I can't give too much away.

"It's controlled remotely," said Ruby, thinking on her feet.

They drove on for another few minutes, with no one talking. Then Danny shouted, "Hey, stop the car!"

The father braked sharply, and Danny got out, taking a few steps up a rise. Jack and Ruby followed. "What's up?" said Jack.

"I heard something," said Danny. "Fire."

Jack's nose smelled smoke and as they reached the crest, he was shocked to see the smouldering remains of *Arrow II* just below.

"That makes no sense," said Ruby.

"We must've been driving in a circle!"

The all turned back to the ATV, but the family were out of the car and standing right behind them. Jack almost jumped out of his skin. *I didn't even hear their footsteps!*

"What's going on?" he asked.

"You need to come with us," said Maxi.

"Uh, I think we should maybe make our own way," said Jack as he exchanged glances with his friends. "Thanks for all your help, though."

"You need to come with us," said Maxi again. She wore a huge fixed smile, but her tone was emotionless.

Something's really wrong here!

"What if we don't want to?" said Danny. Jack realised they'd left their weapons back in the ATV.

"You need to come with us," said the father, grinning too. He reached out and grabbed Ruby by the arm.

"You're hurting me!" said Ruby. She thew her elbow back into the man's chest to get away from him, but the man didn't so much as budge. "Hey!" She stomped on his foot, but the man still didn't react.

"Get off her!" said Danny. He moved to help Ruby, but Maxi suddenly drove her foot into his stomach, doubling him over. Jack was too shocked to react for a second, but then the father began to drag Ruby away. She struggled, but couldn't break free. Jack saw her eyes glowing, but knew she wouldn't use her fire-beams against a normal person.

Maxi scooped Danny up on to her shoulder as if he weighed nothing, and carried him towards the vehicle.

How can she be so strong?

"Don't fight us," said the mother, facing Jack.

"Who are you?" he asked, panicking.

She jabbed at him with her fist and then whipped her leg at him in a vicious roundhouse kick.

"Whoa!" said Jack, ducking to avoid the attack with only centimetres to spare. He didn't want to hurt the woman, but he also didn't want her to knock his head off. "Please, stop!"

She lunged for him, and he dodged to one side. She staggered and fell forward, her head thumping into a rock on the ground. She lay still. Jack sucked in a breath, his heart filling with dread. "Are ... are you OK?"

Fearing the worst, he edged towards her, but in the next moment, the woman rose to her feet in a single, fluid movement. As she turned to face

him, he gasped in shock. Half her
face had gone, and in its place he saw
a mass of alloy plates and complex
wiring. Suddenly, the strange family's
incredible strength made sense.

"They're androids!" he shouted to his
friends.

CHAPTER 5

TERROR IN THE SKY

"ANDROIDS?" ASKED Ruby. "Are you sure?"

"The inside of her head looks like a broken laptop," said Jack.

"Sounds good to me!" Ruby's eyes lit up and she raked a fire-beam into the robot father's chest. Sparks and smoke burst from its clothes and it finally released her, spinning and flailing like a human torch as the flames climbed over its body. Danny was kicking his legs to be free of the Maxi android, but it threw him into the back of the ATV. It was about to slam the door when Danny's sonic burst must have hit it, because it flew through the air, off its feet, and slid across the ground. Danny emerged from the open door, holding their weapons. He tossed Ruby's shield across, and Jack's sword too. The android girl picked itself up, and charged at him again with incredible speed, but he already had an energy arrow nocked to his bow. It hit the Maxi android, flattening her. It fell on the ground with smoke rising from its eyes and mouth, before lying still.

"Short-circuited!" said Danny triumphantly.

The android that looked like a woman ran at Jack, smashing into him and knocking him on to his back. It fell on top, vice-like hands finding his throat and squeezing. Jack gripped its wrists and tried to push it off, but it was strong. One eye gleamed while the other rotated on tiny motors in the exposed socket. Jack concentrated on his hands, letting his super-strength flow into his fingers. He managed to shove it away, then drove his foot into its midriff, and tossed it backwards over his head. As he scrambled to his feet it was already crawling towards him on all fours. Jack took a sidestep and sliced downwards with Blaze, decapitating the robot. Breathing hard, he looked across at his friends. The android that had been made to look like a girl was lying still, and her "dad" had fallen on its side. The fire across its broken pieces was almost out, leaving only charred metal and fried circuitry behind.

"They must be from Cyclops too," said Danny.

"Areevo really doesn't want us getting any closer to the facility," Ruby added.

Jack walked towards the ATV and climbed into the driving seat. "He'll have to try harder next time," he said, and started the engine.

The others got in too, and Danny fished the map from the glove compartment, turning it upside down and around. "Any idea where we are?"

Ruby pointed to another set of tracks on the dusty ground, which must have been made by the ATV when the androids first arrived at the crash.

"I say we follow those," she said. "If these androids came from Cyclops, then those tyre-marks probably lead straight back there."

They drove over the rocky terrain as fast as they dared, following the trail. All the way, Jack's mind went back to the kidnap. All the evidence pointed to Areevo Vaste being responsible, but the question was, why?

What could a billionaire tech genius need his former professor for?

A dark shape appeared on the horizon ahead. Jack gave the ATV more gas. As they approached, the structure in front of them grew. It was a colossal monolith, gleaming a reflective black colour like a giant, polished gemstone. There were no other buildings around it. No fences, or guard towers, or gates. Not even any windows that Jack could see.

"Do we knock?" asked Danny.

"I can't see a door," said Jack.

Suddenly, the ATV's engines died, and it coasted on for a few metres before coming to a halt.

"Is it out of fuel?" said Ruby.

Jack tried to restart the vehicle, with no luck. "It's like it just shut down."

"Uh-oh," said Ruby, pointing upwards.

Jack peered up and saw a flock of the drone-birds detaching from the side of the building, and swooping towards them, circling in perfect formation. Jack guessed there were twenty or so. They were eerily silent, as if waiting for something.

The birds opened their beaks as one, and the serrated tips of their wings began to whirr.

"Maybe they're friendly drones," said Danny hopefully.

Jack shook his head. *We're sitting ducks.*

STORY 2

PROFESSOR RUFUS looked around the huge chamber filled with computers and high-tech equipment. He recognised some — capacitors, electro-magnetic coils, insulating materials. "Where are we?" he asked.

"At Cyclops HQ," said Areevo.

"Why have you kidnapped me? You were always such a nice young man!"

"Sometimes unpleasant things are necessary," said Areevo, "if you want to seize control."

"Control of what?" said Rufus.

Areevo turned away. "Of everything," he said. "For the last year I've watched the leaders of the world

stumble blindly from one crisis to the
next, talking ... always talking ... and
never getting anything done. When
I'm in charge, all that will change."

Rufus couldn't believe what he was
hearing. "That's not the Team Hero
way," he said. "We help people. We

don't control them."

"What's the difference?" scoffed Areevo. He clapped his hands. "To business. I know you've perfected your portal generator at the Academy. I want you to build a replica for me."

Rufus realised now what all the high-tech equipment was for. But there was no way he would build a generator for a madman like Areevo. In the wrong hands, its power source would be a devastating weapon.

"I refuse!" he said.

Areevo turned back to him. "I thought you might say that. However, I'll invite you to reconsider."

"Team Hero will find me," said Rufus. "They'll stop you."

Areevo's laughter echoed through the chamber. He pointed to a screen, where an image flickered into life. It showed Jack, Ruby and Danny in some sort of vehicle, while terrifying bird-like drones circled them like a deadly tornado. Rufus could see the terror etched on the children's faces. They were hopelessly outnumbered.

"Unless you want to see your precious students diced into pieces, I suggest you get building," said Areevo.

Trembling with fear, Professor Rufus nodded.

CHAPTER 1

CYCLOPS HQ

"I'M PRETTY sure they're not friendly," said Ruby. The circle of drone birds, saw-feathers spinning, was closing in on the car where they sat.

It's almost as if they're toying with us, thought Jack. He tried the ATV's ignition again, but nothing happened.

"Well, I'm not planning on just

letting those birds cut us to bits," said Danny. "Let's fight back!"

"Agreed," said Ruby.

Jack put his hand on the car door, looking towards the towering Cyclops Security building, maybe fifty paces away. There was no obvious way in. "If we can get inside, we might be able to barricade ourselves somewhere safe," he said.

They scrambled out, and straight away, the drones descended. Jack smashed two with Blaze, and Ruby drove another back with her shield. Her fire-beams criss-crossed the sky back and forth. Danny fired

two arrows at once, sending two
drones spinning out of control and
careening into a third. Jack ducked
as a serrated wing passed horribly
close to his head. He saw a bird diving
towards Ruby's blindside and called

out a warning. At the last moment
she spun around and the drone
thumped into her shield, exploding on
impact. For every bot they put down,
more seemed to appear in its place.
Danny sonic-blasted several, but they
regrouped and flew at him in unison.
He struggled to line up an arrow, but
Jack saw there was no way he could
take all of them out at once. He ran
at his friend and shoulder-barged him
momentarily out of danger. One of
the drones flew straight into the ATV,
with a crash of metal on metal.

It gave him an idea.

"Keep them busy!" said Jack, diving

under the car. The drones were too big to fit beneath, and broke away to focus on his friends.

Ruby bobbed and weaved as two drones came at her. She zapped them both into flames. Danny sent out a few more sonic blasts from behind the safely of Ruby's shield.

"Now isn't the time to hide!" Danny shouted.

I'm not hiding, thought Jack.

He waited until he was sure the coast was clear, then rolled on to his back. His hands glowed gold as he gripped the axle between the two front wheels. With a heave, he hoisted

the ATV upwards, then climbed to his feet. His arms shook with the weight of the vehicle, but he managed to take one step, then two, while holding it aloft. His friends were still fending off the drones. Jack picked up his pace towards the Cyclops HQ, the car above his head. When he was ten metres away, he hurled the vehicle with a roar of effort. The ATV crashed into the black glass wall, shattering a section.

"Get inside!" he called to the others. "Quickly."

Sheltering behind Ruby's shield, they ran from the flock of drones, returning fire when they could with arrows and fire-beams. Jack came to their side, slashing and stabbing with Blaze. At the smashed section of the glass wall, Ruby and Danny slipped through. Jack went last,

gripping the wreck of the ATV
and hauling it behind him to plug
the hole in the glass. They found
themselves in a giant, empty atrium
full of dying plants. As Jack had
suspected, the thick glass was one-
way, and they could see clearly
through to the outside, where drones
flung themselves into the panes with
no effect. One or two suctioned on,
and began to use their saw-wings
to attack the glass. Others were
attacking the ATV, grinding through
the metal carcass of the car.

"It won't be long until they're
through," said Ruby. "Let's go!"

They crossed the lobby of the building. There was a reception desk, and a security gate with scanners, but no one manning either.

"Where is everyone?" asked Danny.

Jack felt a sense of dread stealing over his skin. He stopped at the desk and ran his finger through a thick layer of dust. "I don't think anyone's been here for quite a while," he said.

"But that's crazy," said Ruby. "Cyclops Security is a huge company! Thousands of people must work here!"

"Let's just hope they're OK," said Jack. He went across to the directory board near the elevators. There were

floors for Research and Development, Accounts, Security, a restaurant and gym, meeting rooms and a boardroom, and several other departments.

Areevo could have Professor Rufus anywhere in the building.

Ruby stabbed the elevator's call button, but nothing happened. "It's not operating," she said. "Maybe there

are emergency stairs." Behind them, the first of the drones were almost through the glass.

Suddenly, the elevator doors opened. Jack, Danny and Ruby tumbled inside. With a scatter of broken glass, the first drone flew into the lobby, followed by a flood of others. Their red eyes settled on Jack and his friends.

Danny frantically hit the buttons, but none of them worked.

The drones all darted towards them at once. Jack raised his sword, and Danny strung his bow. They were trapped in the tiny elevator, ready for a final stand.

Just as it looked like the drones would reach them, the doors slid closed.

"Phew!" said Danny, as the lift began to descend. "That was close!"

"Which floor did you press?" asked Ruby.

"All of them," Danny replied.

Jack saw there was a single basement level, but the elevator seemed to be dropping quickly, going far deeper than a single storey below ground.

"I've got a bad feeling about this," he said, as they sank into the depths of Cyclops HQ.

We're on Areevo's turf now ...

CHAPTER 2

AREEVO'S LAB

THE ELEVATOR came to a halt on a level that wasn't marked on the elevator's display.

The doors opened on to a cavernous space. Jack guessed it was the length and width of a football pitch, if not larger. Gantries ringed the perimeter, but the space in the centre looked like a cross between a mechanic's workshop and a laboratory. Vast pieces of hydraulic machinery sat alongside computing desks. There were thick industrial cables, but also microscopes and holographic modelling displays, servers and screens. It looked like an inventor's paradise.

And there, working at the centre of it all, was Professor Rufus. He was leaning over what appeared to be a dome-shaped contraption. He wore a head-torch and held a tablet in one hand, and some sort of electrical welding tool in the other.

"Professor!" cried Danny.

Rufus looked up, and Jack saw fear in his tired features, then relief. "You're alive!" he said. "Thank goodness!" He cast a glance around. "But you must be careful. He'll be back, at any moment—"

"He's back already," said a voice from somewhere above.

Jack looked up and saw Areevo Vaste on the next platform up.

"I must say, you three are very resourceful," said the young man. "First you escape the Command Centre, then survive a plane crash, and then finally fight your way past my little pets."

"Why are you doing this?" said Ruby. "You're a graduate of Hero Academy!"

"I've moved on from all that," said Areevo, with a dismissive wave. "My ambitions are aimed rather higher these days."

Jack drew Blaze. "We're stopping you," he said. "And we're taking Professor Rufus back."

Areevo cocked his head. "The dear old Professor has a job to finish first."

Jack was tired of listening to Areevo's smug voice. He descended a set of steps to the level where Rufus was working, along with his friends.

"Jack, no!" said Rufus. "Save yourselves."

"Too late," said Areevo. He lifted his fingers to his lips and let out a shrill whistle. Jack heard the skittering of metal on metal, and a large scorpbot scurried from the side of the lab.

"Allow me," said Danny. He lined up an arrow and fired. The droid ducked and the arrow missed. Danny, frowning, shot again. This time, the scorpion sidestepped deftly.

"They're learning," said Areevo. "Remember, every action you take against one of my droids only adds to their collective intelligence. They get better but, alas, you stay just the same."

Danny opened his mouth and let rip a blast of sound towards the scorpbot. It tried to grip the floor, but the pressure of the sonic wave drove it backwards and slammed it into a computer desk. Before it could find its

feet again, Danny's third arrow sent a ripple of sparks over its metal limbs. It collapsed, smoking and motionless.

"I've still got a few tricks," muttered Danny.

Jack rushed across to Professor Rufus, but before he even reached him, Areevo whistled and scorpbots

surrounded his teacher. Their laser stingers were poised, all aiming at the Professor's head.

"They're networked to think as a team, you see?" said Areevo. "They read each other's minds. You can disarm one, but you can't take on all of them."

"Let him go!" said Danny.

Jack saw that his friend had climbed up to the gantry where Areevo Vaste was standing. He had an arrow pointed right at the Academy graduate.

"Stalemate," said Jack.

Areevo lifted his arms. "Not exactly."

Jack saw a movement in the shadows behind his friend.

"Danny, look out!"

It was too late. A scorpbot headbutted Danny in the side, and sent him tumbling over the gantry. Jack rushed forward, braced himself and caught his friend. They both collapsed in a heap on the ground.

Areevo moved quickly down the metal steps to their level, grabbing what looked like a bazooka on the way. He was halfway through levelling it when Ruby shot a fire-beam that ripped it from his hands. As the smoke cleared, Jack ran

at Areevo and tackled him to the ground. He lifted a fist, the skin glowing, and brought it down. Areevo dodged, and Jack's fist crunched into the floor. Areevo stood up and flexed his shoulders.

"I've heard about those golden

hands," he said, raising his own in a boxer's stance. "Let's see what you're made of!"

"I don't want to hurt you," Jack replied.

Areevo punched him in the nose, bringing stars to Jack's eyes. He jabbed back, but Areevo bobbed away with lightning reflexes. Jack stepped forward, and drove another punch into his midriff. It should have been enough to make even the toughest person double over, but the young man took it.

He expected a bolt of electricity in return — wasn't that Areevo's special power? — but instead, Areevo simply charged. Jack swung a hand to protect himself. It connected with the side of Areevo's head with an odd metallic thump, sending the head flying through the air, leaving a tangle of frayed wires sticking out of

the severed neck, spitting sparks.

Jack gasped.

Areevo's a robot too?

"Is anyone actually a normal person round here?" said Ruby.

Jack's horror was replaced with confusion. The scorpbots surrounding Professor Rufus shut down at once, as if their plugs had been pulled. They must have been somehow linked to the Areevo android.

Jack stepped over the mechanical head of Areevo's doppelganger and bypassed the deactivated scorpbots to reach Professor Rufus. From the look on their teacher's face, Jack guessed he hadn't known Areevo was a robot, either.

"What's going on?" asked Danny.

Professor Rufus was frowning. "He said he wanted me to use my portal technology to create a massive power source. I've no idea why."

"We can work that out later," said Ruby.

They ushered the shaken Professor back towards the elevators.

Suddenly, the scorpbots at their backs began to power up again, finding their feet and turning as one.

"Run!" said Jack.

They were almost at the elevator

when the doors opened and a figure stepped out. Jack skidded to a stop at the shocking sight.

"What the—?" said Danny.

Standing right there was another Areevo Vaste. This one held what looked like a laser blaster in his hand.

"Going somewhere?" he said.

Jack saw the barrel of the weapon flare brightly, and what looked like a net made of light burst towards them. He lifted his arms but as soon as the strands touched him, his body was gripped with an electric charge. He lost control, muscles stiffening, just before everything went dark.

CHAPTER 3

SCORP-X FIGHTS BACK

WHEN JACK woke again, he saw his friends sitting beside him in the gloom. The new Areevo Vaste android stood metres away, smiling smugly. Jack rushed at him, and Ruby yelled "No!" but it was too late to stop. He met a hard, invisible barrier that sent him rocking back, his body filling with pain. A criss-cross of lights fizzed into life briefly then disappeared again.

It's some sort of cage made of electricity!

The pain soon faded, leaving an odd sensation of pins and needles, but Jack didn't fancy trying again.

"Your friends didn't make the same mistake twice," said Areevo. "It's just one of my little inventions. It doesn't matter how strong your hands are — there's no escape."

"Where's Professor Rufus?" said Jack.

"Don't worry about him — he's hard at work," said the android. "If he succeeds, and does my bidding, I might even let you live."

He turned on his heel and disappeared into the darkness.

Jack approached the invisible cell wall again. Taking off his shoe, he tossed it. The "bars" flared once more, and Jack saw they extended at least six metres to a spot high above. The whole cage was shaped a bit like a bell. As the light died, he realised they weren't alone, and his heart spiked in his chest. A figure was crouched across the other side of the strange cell.

"Who are you?" he asked.

His friends started as the figure

stood up, shuffling towards them.
Even with the ragged, filthy clothes
and the bushy, unkempt beard, Jack
recognised him.

"Areevo!" he said.

"I'd like to say the one and only,"

mumbled the man, holding out a hand. "But that's not true any more."

Jack shook the hand and introduced himself and the others. He was shocked at how thin Areevo's wrist was.

"You're real?" said Danny.

Areevo looked down at himself and sighed. "An android would look much more presentable."

"How long have you been down here?" asked Jack.

Areevo shrugged. "Perhaps six months. Scorpbots bring me enough food and water to survive, but I lost count of the days a long time ago."

"What happened?" said Ruby.

The sorry-looking young man looked at them with watery eyes. "I ... miscalculated." He chuckled, but there was no joy in the laughter. "I was working on an AI called Scorp-X that could learn from its experiences and surroundings, that could adapt to new situations, and that could share its wisdom across different networked machines. I never stopped to think what might happen if it became too clever."

"It went rogue," said Danny.

"That's putting it mildly," said Areevo. "Scorp-X decided it didn't need me any more — didn't need humans at all. I woke one day to find it had fired all the staff. I didn't know how at first, until I saw what it had created. A replica of me! And not just one. I don't know how many there are ... They locked me in here."

"We have to escape!" said Jack. "Areevo — I mean, the Scorp-X AI — is using Professor Rufus to build something in the underground lab."

"The professor is here too?" said Areevo, eyes going wide. "This is worse than I thought."

"How do we get out?" said Danny.

Areevo shook his head. "We can't.

The walls of the cage can learn, just like the rest of the AIs. The harder you hit it, the higher the charge that hits you back."

"So how do we cut the power?" asked Ruby.

Areevo pointed upwards to a panel in the ceiling. "The central circuit boards are behind there."

Ruby craned her neck and her eyes flashed as a fire-beam shot straight up. After a few seconds, she switched off the flames. The panel was undamaged.

"It's designed to be tamper-proof," said Areevo. "Trust me, I've tried." He

wiggled his fingers and blue electrical charge danced between them.

"Cool!" said Danny.

"And completely useless," said Areevo. "I can short out any circuit, but that panel doesn't conduct."

"If I could get to the panel, I could probably rip it off," said Jack.

"That would be a great plan," said Areevo. "If you can jump five metres straight up."

Jack looked at his friends, heart sinking. All their special powers, and they were still trapped. But then he had a thought. "I can't jump five metres, but if I stood on all of your shoulders I might be able to reach that far."

From the flash in Areevo's eyes, Jack saw he thought it was possible. "I'm very weak, though," he said. "I don't think I could hold any of you."

Danny tapped Jack's shoulder and crouched. "I'll go at the bottom. Ruby can stand on me, and then you can stand on her."

"It's worth a try," said Ruby. She clambered on to Danny's shoulders, and he straightened up, tottering. Ruby was still well short of the panel.

"Here," said Areevo. "I'll give you a boost, Jack."

Jack put his hands on Areevo's narrow shoulders, his foot on Areevo's hands, and climbed up beside Ruby. *Now for the hard part.*

Areevo helped support Danny at the bottom while Jack took Ruby's arms. She braced against him, while he placed one foot on her hip, then another on her shoulder.

"Can't hold it much longer!" said Danny from the bottom.

Jack managed to balance on Ruby's shoulders, then reached up and hooked his fingers under the panel. Ruby fell away beneath him with a cry, and left him dangling from the ceiling. Jack looked down at his friends, in a heap below.

"Can you pull it off?" called Danny.

Jack felt his scaled hands fill with power, and strained his fingers to breaking point. With a creak, the panel began to give, bending backwards. Suddenly it came loose in his hand

and he plummeted down. Danny and Ruby cushioned his fall, but he still tumbled to the ground with a cry of pain.

"Are you OK?" asked Ruby.

Jack picked himself up. "Nothing broken," he muttered. Between this and the plane crash, he'd be awfully sore tomorrow.

"My turn," said Areevo. He lifted his hand, and a bolt of crackling blue

electricity shot from his fingertips and into the exposed circuit-board. The cage bars flared yellow, then white, then, with a pop, they vanished.

"We did it!" said Danny.

"I've missed this," said Areevo, smiling at the others. "It's like being part of Team Hero again!"

He led them to a set of stairs that descended deep underground. They took flight after flight, until Jack's thighs were burning.

"The building has more levels beneath the ground than above," said Areevo. "I built the place to be as secretive as possible."

Eventually they reached a door that said "Level -30".

"We're here," said Areevo. "Remember, Scorp-X is cleverer than any of us and learning all the time."

"That's reassuring," said Danny.

"We have to work as a team if we're going to defeat it," Areevo added. "Ready?"

They nodded, and went through the door. The lab was just as they'd left it, but android-Areevo and Rufus were standing together, overlooking the dome-like hub in the centre.

"You've arrived just in time to see the next stage," said the robot, who seemed completely unfazed by their arrival. "Tell them, Professor."

Professor Rufus looked utterly defeated. "I'm so sorry," he said. "He said he'd kill all of you if I didn't do what he asked."

"What have you done, Scorp-X?" asked the real Areevo.

"The upgrade is ready," said the android, "thanks to the professor."

He laid a palm on the metal dome, and a series of lights flashed across its surface. Then his body began to judder, and his eyes rolled back in his head. Finally, his knees buckled and he fell to the ground. It looked like the android had malfunctioned.

Did something go wrong? Jack wondered.

But as the ground began to tremble, and Professor Rufus backed away from the dome, Jack realised something truly terrible was about to happen. The lights flickered and dimmed, like the power in the building was draining.

Or being diverted elsewhere ...

The dome began to rise, and as it lifted from the ground, Jack saw it was actually the top of a giant metal head, with a single red eye in the centre of its forehead.

"Oh, great ..." muttered Danny.

Shoulders followed, and then two arms, then another two, each ending in pincer claws that looked like they could crush a small car. Professor Rufus reached their side, and his eyes were fixed on the monstrous form rising into the room. Last of all, a curved tail arched over the creature's head, armed with what looked like a glowing laser blaster. The thing was a cross between a human Cyclops and a scorpion, and its armour gleamed.

The single eye swivelled to look down at them, and Jack felt pinned to the spot. In that gaze he saw

intelligence — cold, mechanical, and
utterly indifferent to human life.

CHAPTER 4

LOOKING DEATH IN THE EYE

"GREETINGS, JACK," boomed a voice from inside the creature. It sounded like Areevo Vaste, only much deeper.

"Is there any way we can stop it?" asked Ruby.

"Can an ant stop an elephant?" asked the giant robot. "For too long, petty humans have held back the tide of progress. Now comes the age of the machine!"

"It likes the sound of its own voice, doesn't it?" muttered Danny.

The massive head turned to face him, and in two bounds its huge robot body reached them. A claw lashed out, and Jack shoved Danny aside. The pincers closed instead on the railings of a gantry and went through the metal like a knife through butter. Jack didn't need to see any more. He lifted Blaze and brought the blade down as hard as he could on the scorpion's leg. The sunsteel made a small dent and bounced off.

"One of the benefits of designing yourself is that no expense is spared," said the android. "My shell is indestructible alloy."

"We'll see about that!" cried Ruby. She ran along the gantry above, shooting fire-beams as she went. The jet of flame arced across the droid's head, leaving a black scar — but no obvious damage.

"I have accessed your Team Hero files," said the robot. "I know your limits, and have none of my own."

The real Areevo stepped up. "This is my problem. Let me handle it."

Jack felt the air near him crackle, and a bolt of jagged blue electricity struck the Cyclops in the centre of its torso. The creature backed away, thrashing its pincer limbs as sparks rippled across its body. Areevo pressed forward, hands outstretched as he delivered thousands of volts from his fingertips.

It's working, thought Jack. *Areevo's winning!*

In the flare of the electric attack, he saw Danny moving Professor Rufus towards the safety of the exit. Suddenly, Areevo sagged to the ground, his power spent. The colossal droid was curled into a ball, its metal shell smoking. Then it slowly got up, its red eye gleaming in triumph.

"Is that all you've got?" asked the Cyclops.

The robot bounded forwards on its hind legs, pincers snapping. Jack dodged as a clawed foot stomped down, and sliced at it with Blaze. The blade had no effect other than sending a jarring impact up his arm. The stinger reared up and pointed at him. Jack rushed between the Cyclops's feet as it stabbed for him, shattering the floor where he'd been standing. Above, Danny roared a

sonic blast that wobbled the giant.
A laser beam from the Cyclops's
eye cut a swathe up towards him.
Danny ducked, but the gantry he was
standing on began to collapse beneath
him. Jack watched in horror as his
friend tumbled off, landing heavily.

"Pathetic," said the Cyclops. "Are
you really the best that Team Hero
has to offer?"

Jack willed power into his hands,
and punched one of the creature's
standing legs. It buckled, and the
massive head swung round. A pincer
snapped towards him, and Jack just
managed to throw up his hands to

block. The creature squeezed, and Jack gritted his teeth, resisting the immense power. His golden hands felt like they were on fire with the effort of keeping the pincer open, and hydraulic fluid leaked from the joint.

Jack locked his eyes with the creature's single hateful stare.

"Is that all you've got?" Jack growled. He saw the stinger tail pointed towards him and pretended he couldn't move.

"Come on, then!" he cried. "Kill me!"

"With pleasure," said the Cyclops calmly. The tail jabbed for him and at the same moment, Jack pushed the claw up. The stinger cleaved into it, and the droid let out a squeal as it pierced its own body. Jack rushed towards where Danny had fallen. Ruby was there already, helping their friend stand up. He had a gash on his arm, but otherwise looked unhurt.

The Cyclops turned to face them all.

"I won't make that mistake again," it said. "Trust me."

Scorpbots flooded from the gantries above, and Jack's heart plummeted.

"I'll deal with them," said Areevo. He directed streaks of electricity at the new threat, frying them on impact. But still more came.

Too many, thought Jack.

Ruby shot fire-beam after fire-beam at any that slipped past, but the tide was getting closer. Danny, still recovering, fired arrows or hurled sonic blasts, scattering the scorpbots.

Jack focused on the Cyclops. Every system had a weakness — he just needed to find it. The whole chamber was filling up with smoke, and he plunged into a cloud, hoping to stay hidden. A scorpbot scurried towards him, but he cut it down with Blaze. Laser beams from other bots targeted him at crazy angles. He ducked under one and jumped another.

The scorpbots are linked to the Cyclops's network, he realised. *They're trying to protect it.* Finally, Jack managed to get underneath the Cyclops, looking for any sign of a switch, or a power socket — any vulnerable point at all. The pincers darted for him. Jack dodged one, but the other caught him in the stomach with astonishing force. The room shot past and Jack thudded into a wall. The impact knocked the breath from his body, and he crumpled in a heap, gasping for air as a pincer hoisted him to a standing position. He tried to push it off, but he was too dazed. Through the smoke, Jack couldn't see his friends at all. Perhaps they'd already been defeated. All he saw was the robot's colossal eye staring at him.

It flared, filling his vision with red as it powered up its laser.

CHAPTER 5

OVERLOAD

AS THE Cyclops's eye laser cut its
deadly path towards Jack, Ruby
suddenly appeared, mirror shield
raised. Jack saw a flash of red and the
pincer released him. He saw the laser
rebounding, striking the Cyclops right
in its eye. It recoiled, pincers smashing
into consoles as it flailed blindly.

Jack used the advantage, running at the creature with Blaze held high. With every last ounce of strength, he cut at one of the joints in the droid's pincer arms. His sword bit down, but the Cyclops jerked the limb back, ripping the sword from his grip and sending Jack sliding across the floor, turning and rolling to get back to his feet. He had drawn up by Areevo, who was still busy fending off the scorpbots.

"It must have a power source," he said.

"I built the internal generator," Professor Rufus called from the doorway. "But it's deep inside its core. There's no way our weapons could ever reach it."

The Cyclops moved towards them, and the air burned as a laser just missed Jack's head. He rolled sideways as another gantry collapsed.

As it did, Jack saw a section of thick electrical cable exposed in the wall. *It must be connected to the building's main supply.*

"I've got an idea," he said. "Ruby, Danny, head for the exit."

"What?" cried Danny. "We can't leave you in here!"

"Trust me," he said. "I've got a plan,

and Areevo will help me."

"You got it," said Ruby. She and Danny backed off, still firing their weapons, towards the door.

"Running away, I see," said the Cyclops. "So much for Team Hero!"

The scorpbots, obeying the Cyclops's silent commands, swarmed after Jack's friends.

Perfect, he thought. He dropped his sword, turned his back on the Cyclops and ran towards the cable, gripping it with both hands and ripping it loose from the wall.

"Come back, Jack," taunted the Cyclops.

Jack instead circled the droid, hauling the cable as he ran. The massive creature maneuvered to face him, and Jack dashed straight between the creature's legs. It reached down, but Jack doubled back again, heading for a set of stairs to an upper floor. Lasers fizzed through the air from the robot's tail and glowing eye, close enough that he could smell the burning dust. Jack jumped off the gantry, landing on the Cyclops's back and sliding off. Then he ran under the legs again. A pincer came for him and he wrapped the cable around it, yanking hard. Slowly but

surely, he was tangling up Scorp-X's
twisted creation. He glanced back
to the room's entrance to see his
friends holding the scorpbots at bay.
Professor Rufus was standing with
them.

"Areevo — get ready!" shouted Jack

"Ready for what?" asked the young man. "You can't just tie it up!"

Jack looped another pincer, then a leg. The Cyclops tottered, then fell on to its side. *That should do it*, thought Jack. He ran towards the others, trampling over the pieces of the scorpbots they'd defeated.

"I need a power surge!" said Jack. "Give me everything you've got, Areevo!"

The inventor looked confused, but Professor Rufus's face lit up. "You're going to overload Scorp-X's core!" he said.

Areevo's eyes widened. "Of course! It

might just work."

Jack brought the end of the cable to him, and Areevo gripped it with both hands. The Cyclops was writhing in the tangles, straining to get free. The other scorpbots swarmed back towards him, and started to cut into the cable with their pincers and drills. It wouldn't be long until their master broke through and resumed his attack. And like he said, he wouldn't show the same weakness a second time.

It's now or never ...

Areevo's whole body shook as he sent electric current through the cable. Blue jolts of power flared from Areevo's hands as the cable vibrated. The lights throughout the room began to dim and flicker as the building's power became unstable.

"More!" cried Rufus.

Computer screens exploded, spitting glass, and Jack felt the hair on his head rising. The Cyclops managed to stand. Lasers from its glowing red eye scoured the walls in random, panicked bursts. The giant robot took a lumbering step towards them, then another.

"You can't do this!" it said. "You can't defeat me. I'm better than you all!"

Areevo's eyes were rolling back in his head and sweat poured from his skin as more and more current left his body and flowed into the jerking cable.

Lights popped into showers of sparks and the humming sound in the air became more like a groan, as if the entire building was roaring out in pain. As the lasers cut into the walls and ceiling, pieces began to break free, crashing below. Red emergency lights flashed and sirens wailed.

"Go!" cried Areevo, still gripping the cable. "The building's coming down! Run while you can."

"We're not leaving you," said Jack.

The Cyclops freed one pincer and reached for Areevo, but then a steel beam fell right on its head and it collapsed to its knees again. It moved weakly, but its red eye dimmed to black as more and more debris showered down, burying it completely. At the same time, the remaining scorpbots simply deactivated and fell down like chunks of scrap metal.

Areevo's power gave up at last, and he staggered back. Ruby and Danny caught him, holding him up, then Rufus beckoned them through the door.

"Everything's collapsing!" shouted the professor. "We have to get out."

"We're thirty floors down!" said Jack.

Areevo pointed with a tired arm

towards a grate in the wall to their left. "That way," he said.

We've got no choice, thought Jack.

Their small party hurried through the wreckage of the chamber to the grate. Jack jammed Blaze into the edge and prised it off. On the other side was a passage lined with pipes and cables. It was only just taller than him, and Areevo and Rufus had to stoop to get in.

"It leads to the outside," said Areevo.

Explosions ripped through the labs at their backs, and the tunnel walls vibrated.

Jack let Areevo lead the way,

followed by the professor and his friends. He went last, plunging into the gloom. Soon the darkness was absolute. He let his hands trail along the rough walls. The only sounds were the gasping breaths of his companions and the shuffle of their footsteps ahead. It was impossible to judge how far they'd come until he saw the faintest of lights ahead and smelled the warm desert air. The outlines of the others became clearer, and then they emerged, blinking, into sunlight. Looking back, Jack saw they'd come from a concrete pipe in the middle of nowhere. Everyone was streaked with sweat, dirt and dust.

But at least we're alive.

"Check it out!" said Ruby.

Jack turned to face the way she was staring and saw smoke billowing from the Cyclops building as explosions ripped from the inside.

"The whole place is going up!" said Danny.

With a thunderous rumble, the building collapsed from the top, floor after floor smashing down into the one below. In just a few seconds, all that remained was a smouldering heap of broken glass and steel. Somewhere far beneath lay the wreckage of the Cyclops and what remained of the

Scorp-X AI.

Areevo watched, his mouth open.

That's his entire life's work, thought Jack.

"It's all right," said Professor Rufus. He put a hand on his former pupil's shoulder. "You can rebuild."

"Just maybe steer clear of AI for a while," said Ruby.

Areevo nodded slowly. "I only ever wanted to help Team Hero," he said.

"We know that," said Jack. "No one blames you for what happened."

Danny shot a glance at Jack and mouthed, "We don't?"

Jack shrugged. There was no doubt that Areevo Vaste was a good person, and a genius. And something told Jack that he'd be a lot more cautious from now on.

"Did I miss something?" asked Hawk in Jack's ear.

"Oh, you're back to normal?" said Jack. "That must mean the Team Hero systems have been restored."

"Message from Command Centre," said Hawk. *"Patching it through to all your Oracles."*

Chancellor Rex's voice came over the intercom system. "Jack!" he said. "What happened? Are you and Ruby and Danny all right?"

Jack looked at the pall of ashy smoke drifting over the remains of Cyclops Security. They'd been lucky to make it out alive.

"We're fine," he said. "There's a lot to explain, but the important part is that we have Areevo and the professor with us." The desert stretched in all directions for miles. "We might need a ride home, though."

"Stand by," said Rex. "We'll send *Arrow II* to your location."

Jack saw Danny swallow.

"Er ... about *Arrow II*, Chancellor," he said, aiming a rueful grin at his two friends. "There might be a small problem ..."

THE END

READ ON FOR A
SNEAK PEEK AT THE
NEXT BOOK:

THE SECRET JUNGLE

CHAPTER 1

INTO THE JUNGLE

IN THE Hero Academy Command
Centre, the main monitor had been
playing Dr Jabari's message on loop
for the last ten minutes. Jack watched
carefully, while also keeping an eye on
his friend Ruby. Danny had an arm
around her shoulders. Though she was
obviously upset, her eyes glinted with

determination. Jack's heart ached for her. He knew what it was like to see your parents in danger.

Also standing before the bank of terminals and screens were Chancellor Rex, the Academy's head, and their tutors, Professor Rufus and Professor Yokata. All of them looked deeply concerned.

Ruby slammed a hand on the control panel, pausing the footage.

'We've got to do something!' she said.

Professor Yokata nodded gravely. 'And we will, Ruby,' he said. 'Though we have to know what we're dealing with.'

'Where is this Taah Lu temple Dr. Jabari was investigating?' asked Jack.

'The Parracudo Jungle,' said Chancellor Rex. 'One of the last great wildernesses on our planet. The Taah Lu were an ancient civilization who stood against the High Command's attacks.'

'They fought General Gore?' asked Danny.

Check out
THE SECRET JUNGLE
to find out what happens next!

READ MORE FROM
ADAM BLADE IN:

BeastQuest

www.beastquest.co.uk